Hands
Say
Love

by George Shannon

illustrated by Taeeun Yoo

L B

Little, Brown and Company
New York   Boston

Hands that do all they can do
are also saying "I love you."

Hands that gently wake you up.

Hands that fill a special cup.

Hands that help the baby walk.

Hands that make a puppet talk.

Pick up blocks.

Match the socks.

Tie a shoe.

Peekaboo!

Hands that dig the garden weeds.
Hands that help to plant the seeds.

Hands that pull a splinter out.

Hands that hold when you're in doubt.

Wipe a tear.
Hold you near.

Toss a ball.
Stop your fall.

Hands that do all they can do
are also saying "I love you."

Hands that help to stir and bake.

Hands that decorate the cake.

Hands that hold a bite to share.
Hands that bring the silverware.

Make a gift.
Help you lift.

Fold a hat.

Pet the cat.

Hands that wave
and wave "Hello!"

Hands that mark how tall you grow.

Hands that tickle someone's chin.
Hands that help you dance and spin.

Play a song.
Clap along.

Sweep the broom.

Clean the room.

Hands that hold a book to share.

Hands that brush
and braid your hair.

Hands that pull the covers tight.

Hands that send a kiss good-night.

Hands that do all they can do
are also saying "I love you."